This is
Poppy.

This is
Max.

When Poppy grows up
she wants to...

When Poppy and Max Grow Up

Lindsey Gardiner

To John with love –
thank you for being you

little ORCHARD

ORCHARD BOOKS
96 Leonard Street London EC2A 4XD
Orchard Books Australia
Unit 31/56 O'Riordan Street, Alexandria, NSW 2015
ISBN 1 84121 699 2 (hardback)
ISBN 1 84121 076 5 (paperback)
First published in Great Britain in 2001
First paperback publication in 2002
Text and illustrations © Lindsey Gardiner 2001
The right of Lindsey Gardiner to be identified as the author
and illustrator of this work has been asserted by her in
accordance with the Copyright, Designs and Patents Act, 1988.
A CIP catalogue record for this book is available from the British Library.
1 2 3 4 5 6 7 8 9 10 (hardback)
1 2 3 4 5 6 7 8 9 10 (paperback)
Printed in Singapore

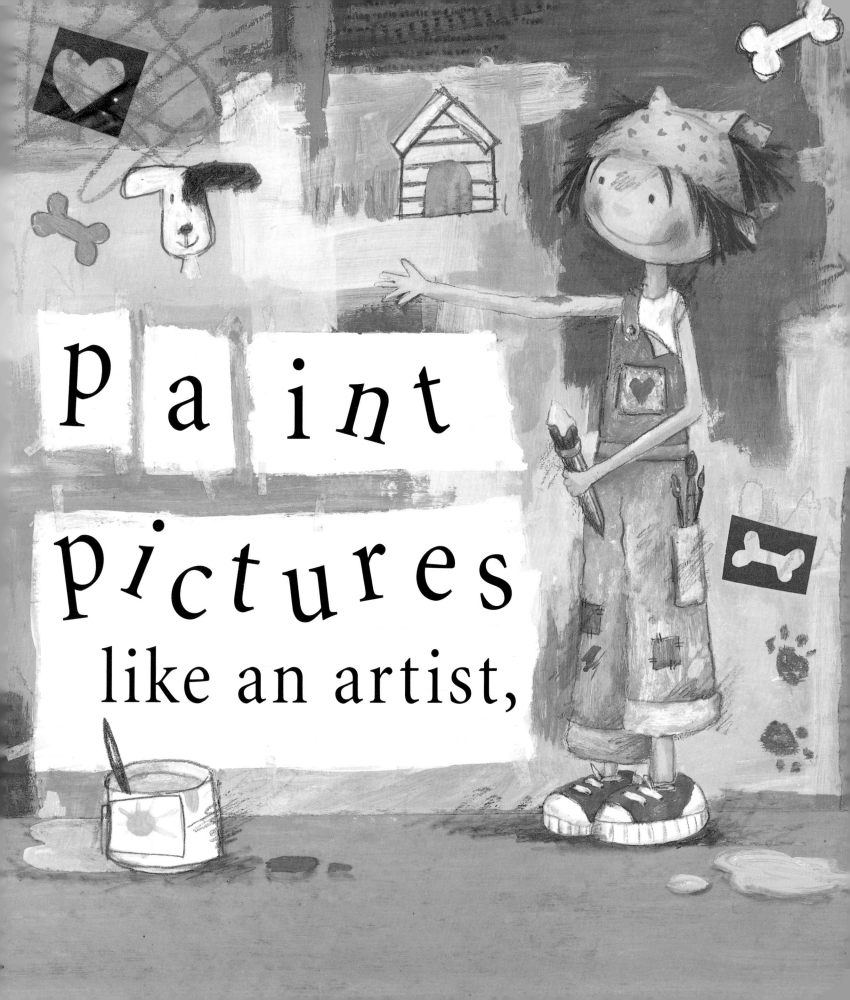

paint
pictures
like an artist,

score

goals

like a footballer,

spin

round

like a ballet dancer,

take

care of sick animals

like a vet,

and dance

like a
pop
star,

cook
yummy
dinners

like a chef,

swim in the

deep sea

like a diver, but...

...right now
Poppy has the best job in the world...

looking after Max.

Bye
bye

See you again soon. . .